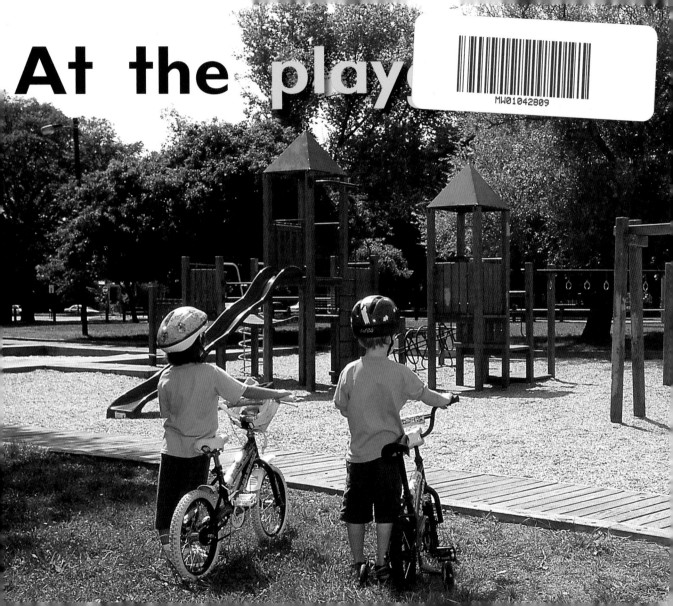

At the play

We are going

on the swings.

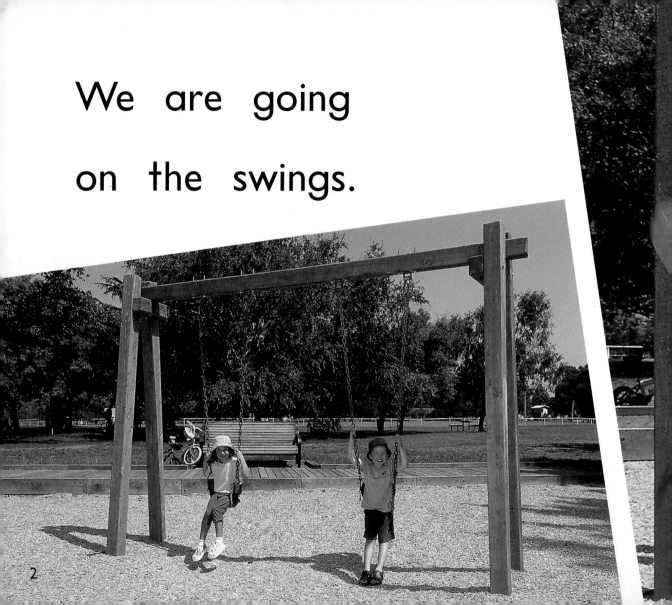

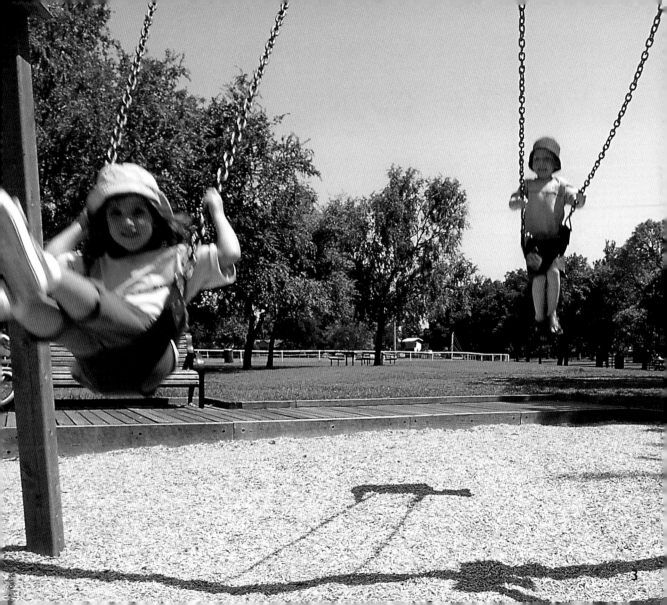

We are going

on the slide.

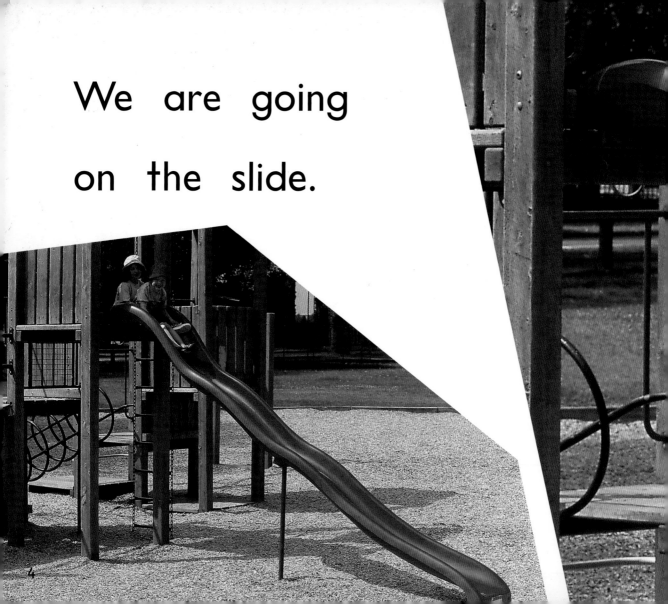

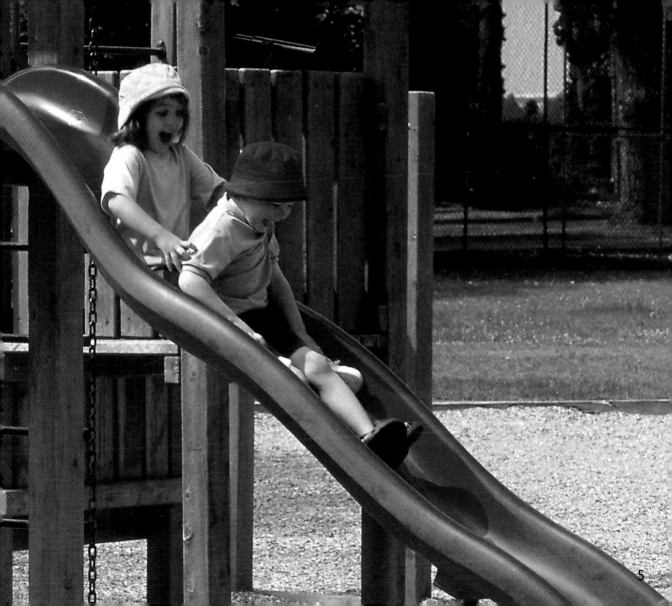

We are going

on the ladder.

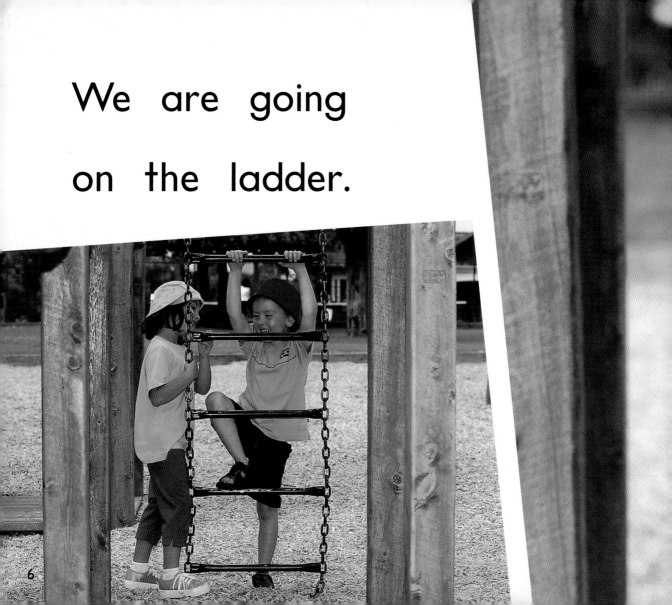

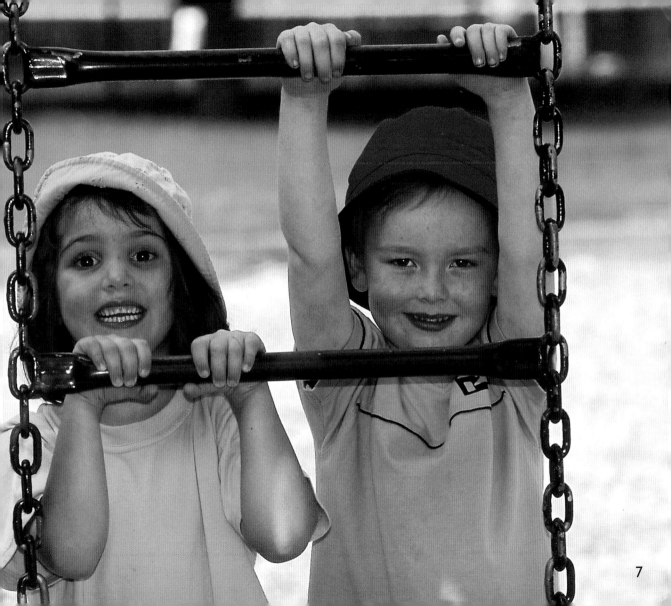

We are going

on the see-saw.

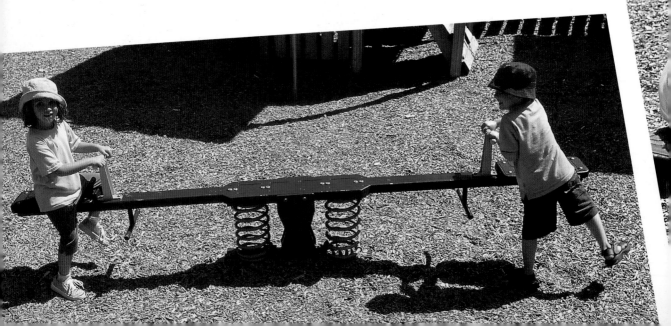

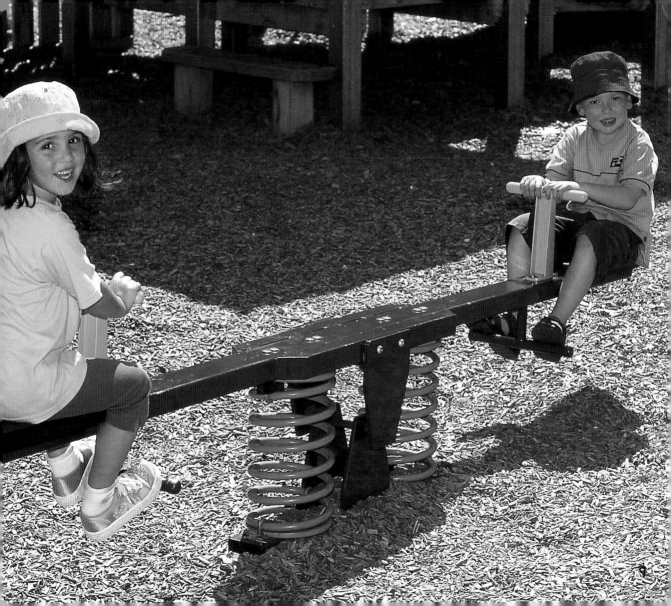

We are going

on the horses.

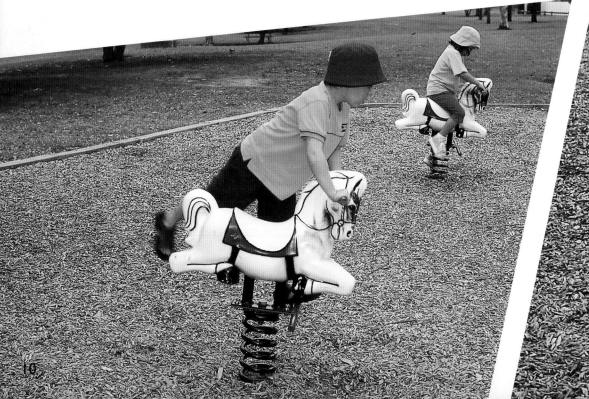

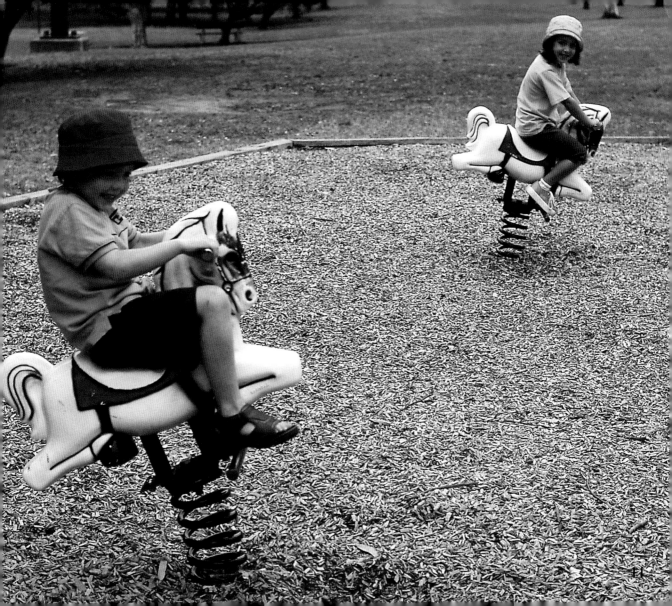

We are going

on the bar.

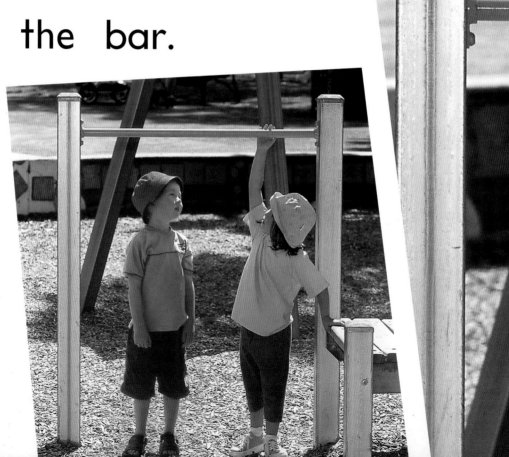

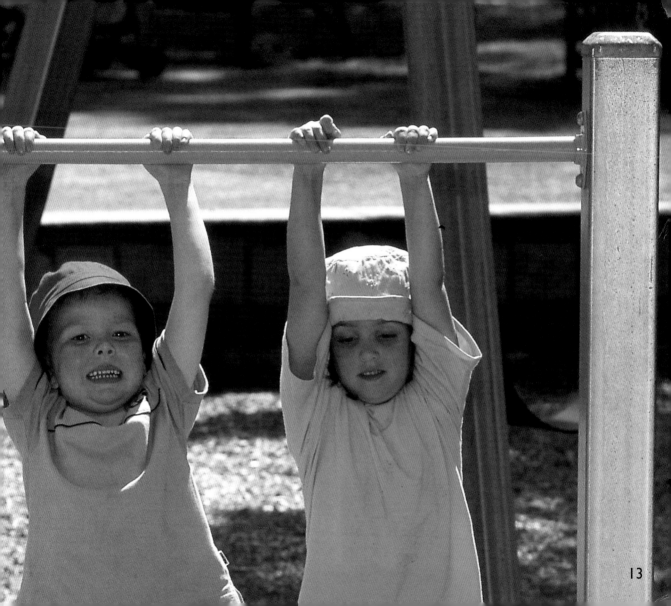

We are going

on the bridge.

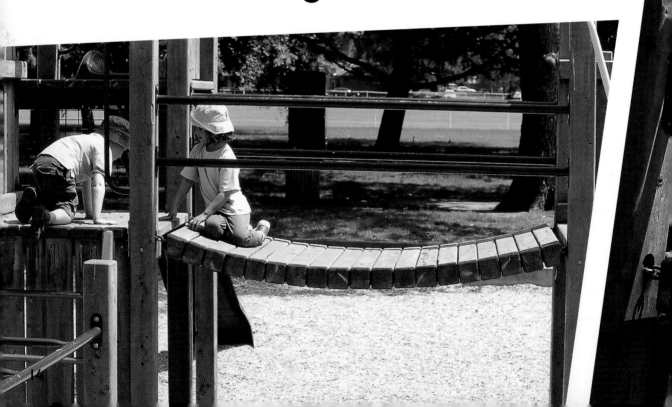

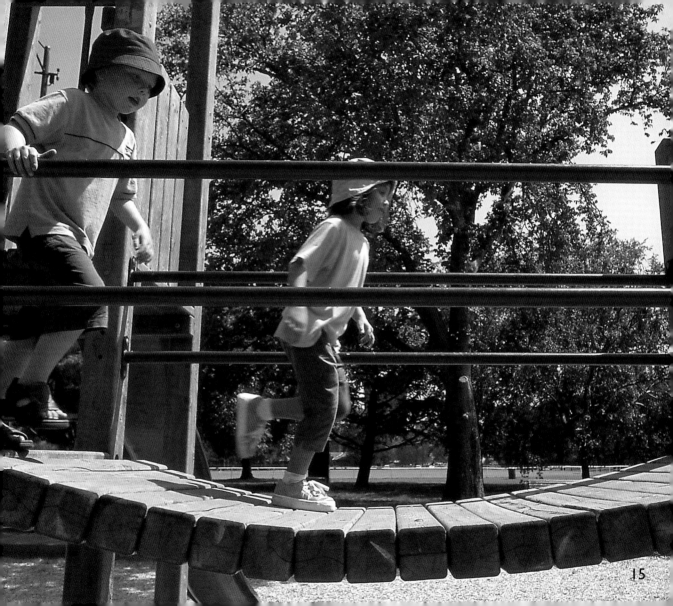

We are going

on the bikes.

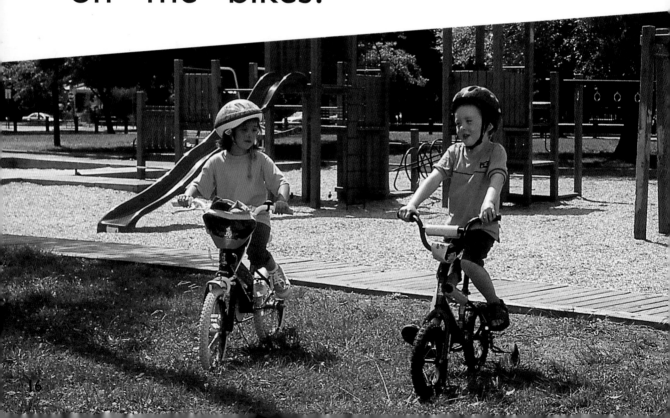